SIMON & SCHUSTER BOOKS FOR YOUNG READERS
An imprint of Simon & Schuster Children's Publishing Division
1230 Avenue of the Americas, New York, New York 10020
Text copyright © 2003 by Robert Kinerk
Illustrations copyright © 2003 by Steven Kellogg
All rights reserved, including the right of reproduction
in whole or in part in any form.
SIMON & SCHUSTER BOOKS FOR YOUNG READERS
is a trademark of Simon & Schuster.
Book design by Dan Potash and Judythe Sieck.
The text for this book is set in Lomba.
The illustrations for this book are rendered in mixed water-based mediums.
Manufactured in China
10 9 8 7 6 5 4 3 2 1
Library of Congress Cataloging-in-Publication Data
Kinerk, Robert. Clorinda / Robert Kinerk ; illustrated by Steven Kellogg.
p. cm. "A Paula Wiseman Book." Summary: Defying the odds,
Clorinda the cow follows her dream of becoming a ballet dancer.
ISBN 0-689-86449-3 [1. Cows—Fiction. 2. Ballet dancing—Fiction. 3. Perseverance
(Fiction)—Fiction. 4. Stories in rhyme.] I. Kellogg, Steven, ill. II. Title.
PZ8.3.K566Cl 2003 [E]—dc21   2003004559

For my mom, Nell Kinerk—R. K.

To Esmé, with love—S. K.

Clorinda

YES! It's the BALLET TODAY!

by Robert Kinerk
illustrated by Steven Kellogg

A PAULA WISEMAN BOOK
Simon & Schuster Books for Young Readers
New York London Toronto Sydney Singapore

A cow named Clorinda, whose farm was remote,
would drive into town each November to vote.
But one year she happened, through some odd mischance,
to sit through a program of classical dance.

Super!
Marvelous!
Magnificent!
WOW!

"I'd like to try that myself," said the cow.

She asked a young farmhand
named Leonard P. Cage
to build, in the back of the barn,
a small stage.

And there, behind tractors
and old stacks of hay,
she put on a tutu
and practiced ballet.

"You can't dance! Are you nuts!" said a turkey named Doris.
The ducks, geese, and hens, in a sort of chorus,
all said to Clorinda, "No, no. That won't do.
You're only a cow, and what *they* do is MOO!"

"Those critics!" scoffed Len.
"Just tell them moo-POOH.
A person can't know
what it is she can do.
Be bold and imaginative!
Shoot for the sky!
If it's dance that you love,
then it's dance you should try!"

Yes! cried Clorinda. And then, for long days,
she practiced her leaps and she practiced jetés.
At last she told Len, "Well, the next step is clear.
I'm off to New York. I must start my career."
"I'll help!" exclaimed Len. "Here's some cash for the flight!"
"Thank you," she said, and she took off that night.

Brilliant Manhattan!
She felt her heart pound.
She rented a walk-up,
and then went around
with other young hopefuls
who lined up each day
in search of a place
in a corps de ballet.

They lined up . . . and lined up . . .

and lined up each day

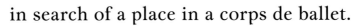

in search of a place in a corps de ballet.

Brutal Manhattan! She felt her heart throb.
She looked at her checkbook—then looked for a job.
"Buck up!" she thought, "for you know that it's true—
a person can't tell what a person can do!
Don't be discouraged. Don't sit down and cry.
Get out there, Clorinda, and give it a try."

SMILE!

She pounded the pavement for day after day,
till finally she found, in a tiny café,
a job waiting tables and cleaning up spills.
Her boss told her, "Smile when presenting the bills."

"KEEP SMILING," she thought, "as you search for the chance

to prove to the world that you really can dance."

"KEEP SMILING," she sobbed, "as you constantly hear,

'We simply aren't hiring cows now, my dear.'"

Poor Len was distressed
when he read in her letter,
"Life cannot get worse—
it can only get better."

And better it got!
The very next day
a theatrical agent
was in the café!
Clorinda's heart leaped
when the fact was disclosed
that a dancer he'd hired
was now indisposed.

"Indisposed?" thought Clorinda.
"Why, this must be fate!"
She spun as she stepped up
and took the man's plate.
She brought him his coffee
on high tippy toes
and glided away
just like someone who knows
pirouetting and leaping
and all about dance.

And the next thing you know, she had her big chance!

Len was the first one she phoned up to tell,
"Tonight I'm on stage in the ballet *Giselle*!"

She rushed off to practice—she practiced all day:

en barre,

her positions,

1st position

2nd position

3rd position

4th position

5th position

and of course, her jeté.

But one leap she feared would be quite hard to do,
for she had to be caught by a dancer named Lou.
She studied her partner, then told him, "Somehow,
you may want to think twice about catching a cow."

"No problem," Lou told her.
He said to her, "Please!
Check out my biceps,
and check out my knees!

I'm in perfect condition, and trained, furthermore,
in helping my partners glide safe to the floor."

"Well, fine then—we'll try it,"
Clorinda replied.
"People can't tell,
at least not till they've tried,
what it is they can do.
And that is a fact."
The stagehands hissed, "HURRY,
you'll miss the first act!"

Sparkling and swirling, the dancers took flight.
The music, the costumes, the dazzling light,

the grace and the glamour, the shouts of "Bravo!"
filled her whole heart with a wonderful glow.

She danced like a feather.
She danced like a flame.

She skipped and she whirled—until the time came for each ballerina to fly through the air,

arc, and float downward, and come to earth, where

their partners awaited
in perfect array
to step forth
and catch them
and dance them away.

Those ahead of Clorinda flew just like a cloud.
The applause that exploded was fervent and loud.

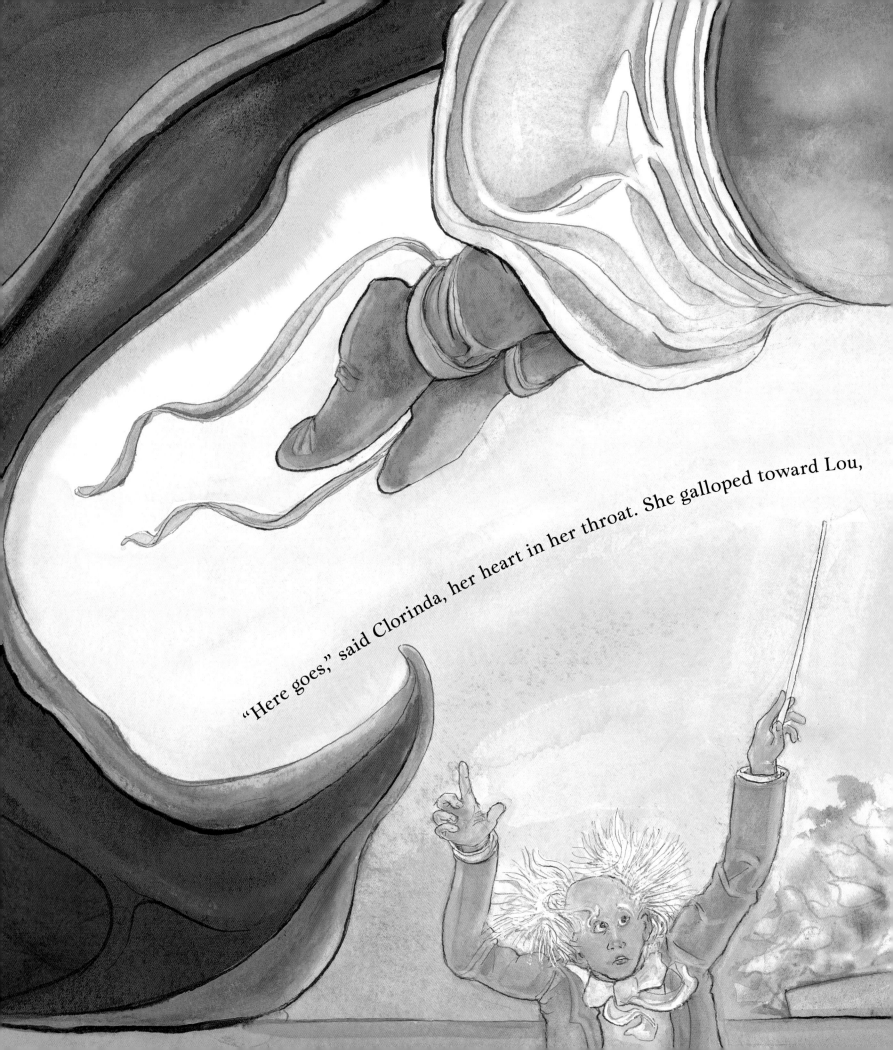

"Here goes," said Clorinda, her heart in her throat. She galloped toward Lou,

then sprang upward to float—to fly like a bird does, as butterflies do.

But the opposite happened—she flattened poor Lou.

She crashed and she smashed and she crushed and she smushed.
And the whole auditorium suddenly hushed.

Oof! Lou gasped weakly. He struggled to rise.

Clorinda was stunned. There were tears in her eyes.
She wished that the stage would just open up wide
so she could be swallowed and hidden inside.

MOOF!

moaned Clorinda.
She straightened a strap.

Then, to her surprise,
she heard somebody clap!

One person started, then row after row
was clapping and cheering and shouting, "Bravo!"

"Why are they clapping—for us?" the cow said.
"It seems that they ought to be booing instead."

"Oh no, Clorinda," Lou said. "In no way!
They all understand that we blew it, but—hey!
They're cheering.
They're shouting.
They're clapping their hands!
They're doing all this because each understands
the thing most important is making a try—
you can't always triumph. You can't always fly.

"We gave it our best, but there's bound to be misses—
Now let's take a bow and let's blow them some kisses!"

Which they did. Then she told him, "You're kind, but it's clear—
it's time that I looked for a different career."

Hugs were exchanged with the cast and the crew.

Clorinda called home and that night she flew
back to the farm and to Leonard P. Cage.

She was moved when she found he'd enlarged her old stage.

"You're a prince, Len," she whispered.

"I'll dance you my thanks."

Then nimbly she mounted those dusty old planks.

She danced like a feather.
She danced like a flame.

Word spread to the neighbors. The animals came.
They clapped for Clorinda. They shouted their praise.

Then over the course of the next several days,
on that stage in the barn behind old stacks of hay,
the marvelous cow trained them all in ballet.

And now if you go there—and don't miss the chance!—
you'll see animals everywhere dance, dance, dance, DANCE!